For Brian and Daphne

This edition is
published and distributed
exclusively by
DISCOVERY TOYS
Martinez, CA

Originally published by
Walker Books, Ltd.
London

© 1988 Penny Dale

Printed in Hong Kong

First American edition

ISBN 0-939979-10-1

TEN·IN·THE·BED

Penny Dale

DISCOVERY TOYS

There were ten in the bed and the little one said,
"Roll over, roll over!"

So they all rolled over and Hedgehog fell out . . . BUMP!

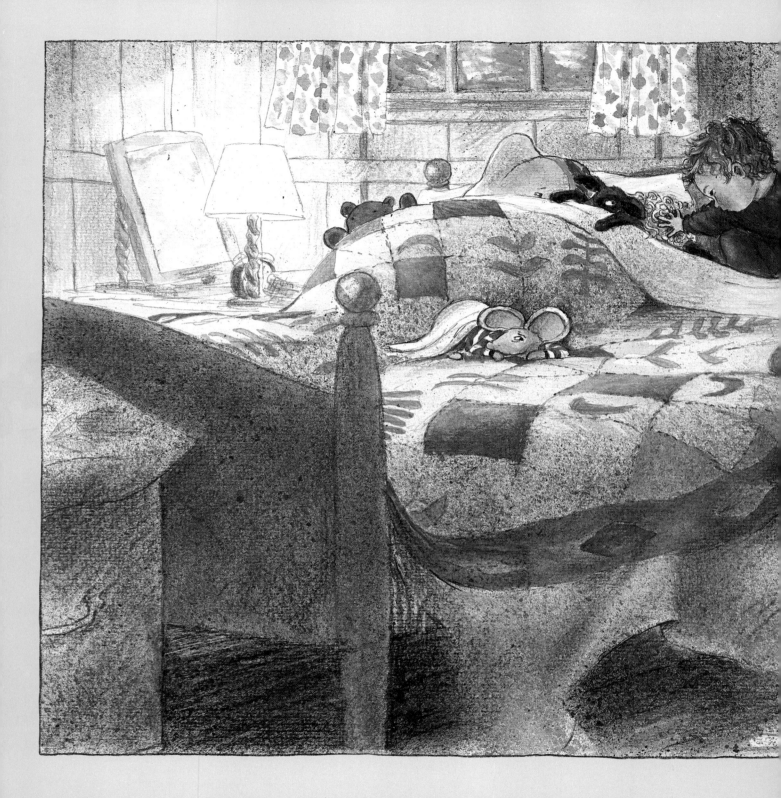

There were nine in the bed and the little one said,
"Roll over, roll over!"
So they all rolled over and Zebra fell out . . . OUCH!

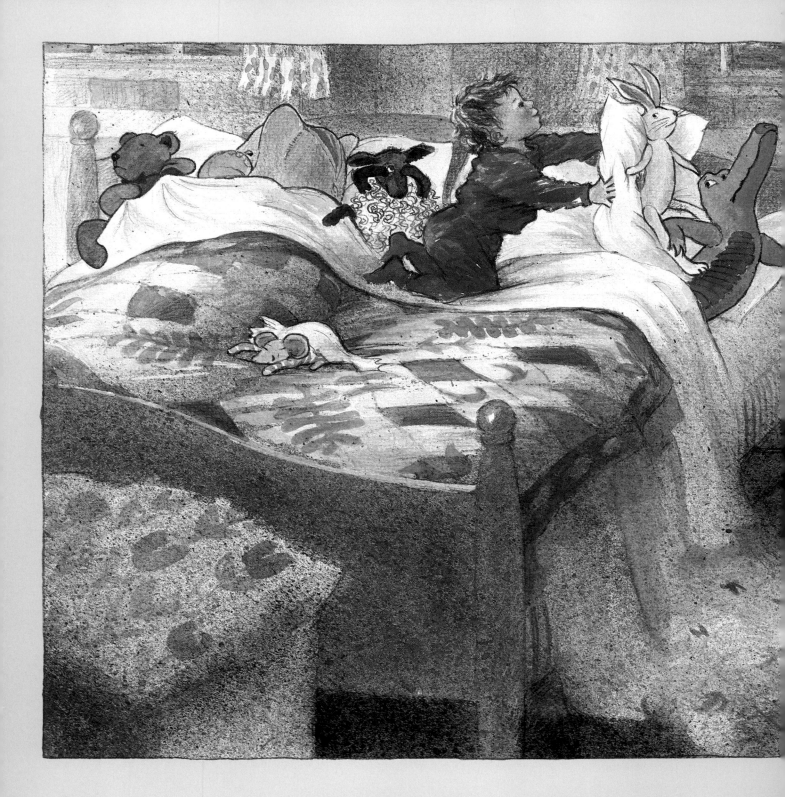

There were eight in the bed and the little one said,
"Roll over, roll over!"
So they all rolled over and Ted fell out . . . THUMP!

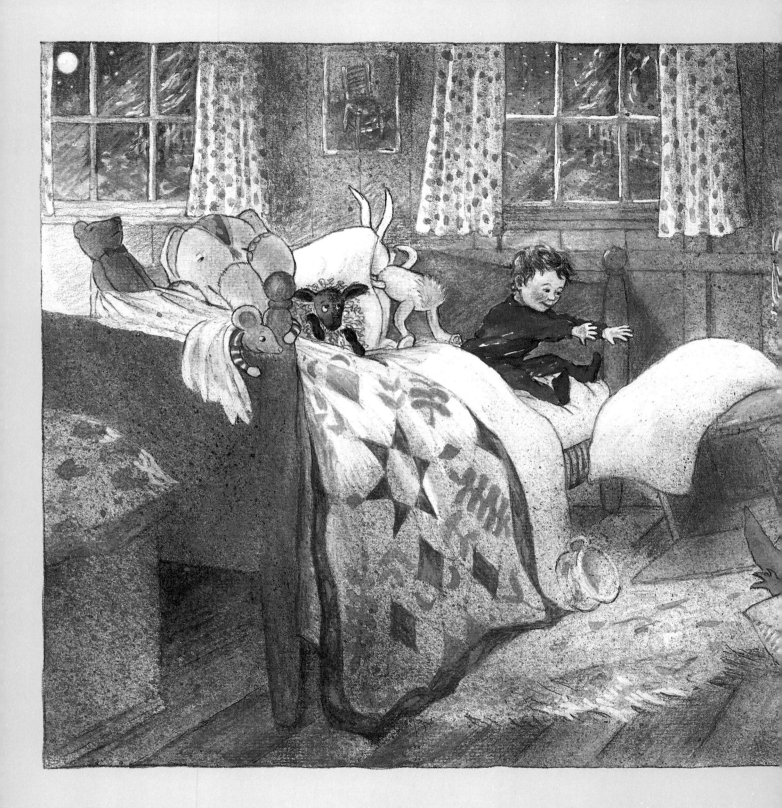

There were seven in the bed and the little one said,
"Roll over, roll over!"
So they all rolled over and Croc fell out . . . THUD!

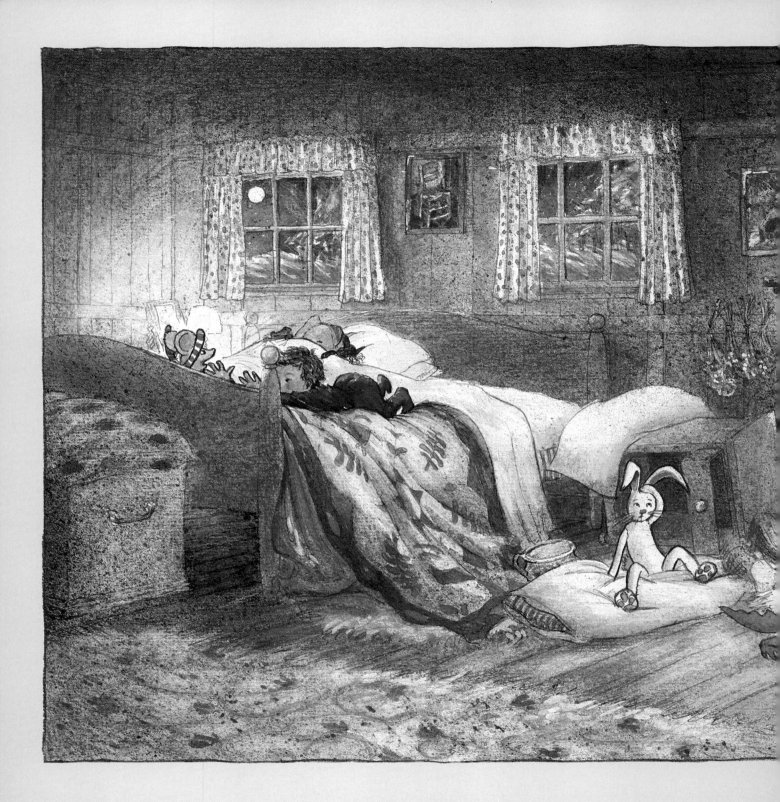

There were six in the bed and the little one said,
"Roll over, roll over!"
So they all rolled over and Rabbit fell out . . . BONK!

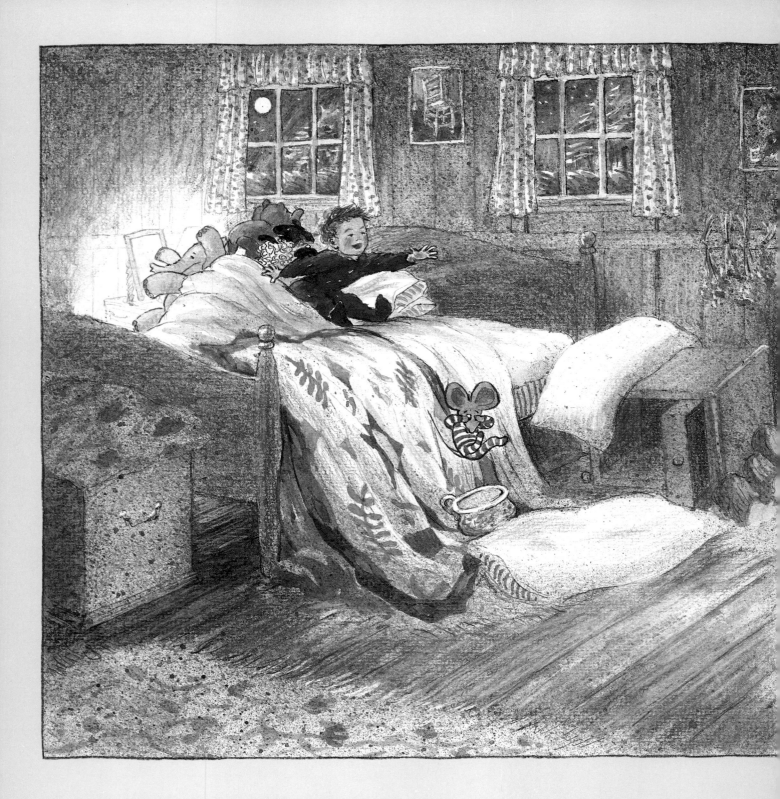

There were five in the bed and the little one said,
"Roll over, roll over!"
So they all rolled over and Mouse fell out . . . DINK!

There were four in the bed and the little one said,
"Roll over, roll over!"
So they all rolled over and Nelly fell out . . . CRASH!

There were three in the bed and the little one said,
"Roll over, roll over!"
So they all rolled over and Bear fell out . . . SLAM!

There were two in the bed and the little one said,
"Roll over, roll over!"
So they all rolled over and Sheep fell out . . . DONK!

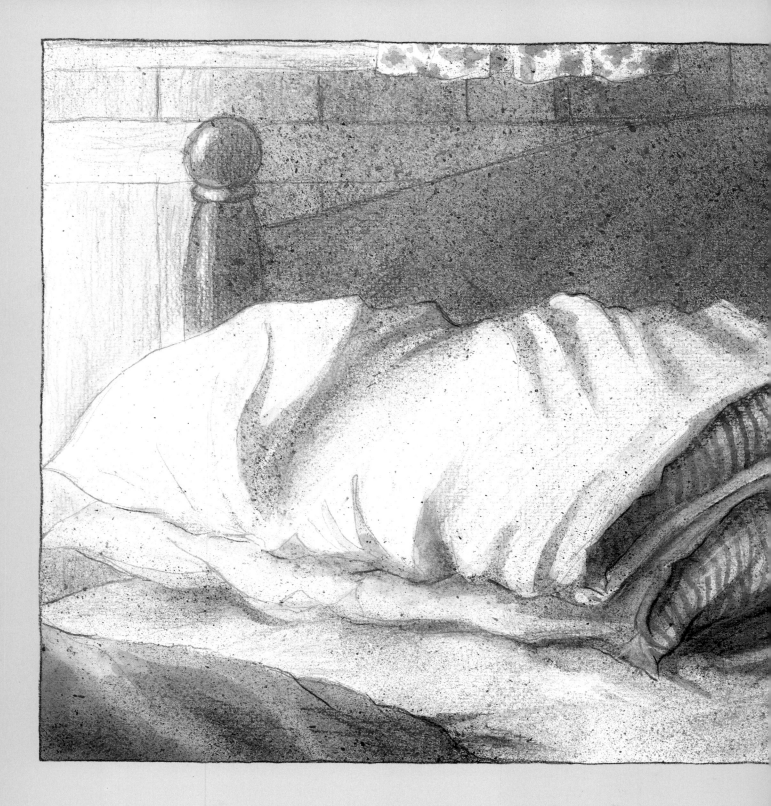

There was one in the bed and the little one said,

"I'm cold! I miss you!"

So they all came back . . .

and jumped into bed – Hedgehog, Mouse,
Nelly, Zebra, Ted,

the little one, Rabbit,
Croc, Bear and Sheep.

Ten in the bed, all fast asleep.

The End